Hans Fischer

In Fairyland

The finest of tales by the Brothers Grimm

North
South

Table of Contents

The Musicians of Bremen

There once was a farmer who owned a donkey that for many long years had faithfully carried his sacks of corn to the mill. But the donkey had become old and weak, and less and less able to do the work, and so his master decided to get rid of him. The donkey realized that something bad was about to happen and ran away. He headed for the city of Bremen, where he thought he might be able to start a new career as a musician.

After he'd been traveling for a while, he came upon a hunting dog who was lying on the path panting as if he'd just run a hundred miles. "Hello, Fox-Chaser," said the donkey, "why are you panting like that?" "Ugh, ugh, ouf!" said the dog. "It's because I'm old, and I'm getting weaker every day, and I can't go hunting anymore. My master was going to beat me to death, so I ran away, but how am I going to earn a living now?" "I'll tell you how," said the donkey. "I'm going to Bremen to be a musician, so come with me and we'll make music together. I'll play the drums and you can blow the trumpet." The dog liked the idea, and the two of them set off together.

Not long afterward they saw a cat sitting on the path with a face as miserable as a wet and windy winter's day. "Hello, Whiskerlicker," said the donkey, "what's got you so down in the dumps?" "Nothing to be cheerful about if you're in my situation," replied the cat. "I'm old, my teeth are blunt, and all I can do is sit by the fire and purr instead of what I should be doing, which is hunting mice. My mistress was going to drown me, but I managed to get away. Now what am I going to do? And where can I go?" "Come with us to Bremen," said the donkey. "You're good at making night music, so you can become a musician." The cat liked the idea, and the three of them set off together.

The three runaways soon came to a farmyard, and on the gate sat a rooster who was crowing with all his might. "What a racket!" complained the donkey. "What are you screaming about?" "I'd just forecast fine weather," said the rooster, "so the mistress could wash and dry the shirts, but there are guests coming tomorrow, and the cruel woman told the cook to make soup out of me for them to eat. They're going to cut my head off tonight, so I'm screaming as loud as I can as long as I can." "That's terrible, Red Rooster," said the donkey. "You'd better come with us. We're going to Bremen. And wherever you go will be better than here and certain death. You've got a good voice, and if we all make music together, it's sure to sound special." The rooster liked the idea, and the four of them set off together.

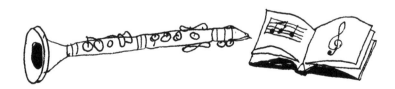

There was no way they could reach Bremen in a single day, and so when it began to get dark, they went into the forest to spend the night there.

The donkey and the dog stretched out under a large tree, and the cat and the rooster went up into the branches—though the rooster flew to the very top as he felt safer there. Before going to sleep, he looked round in all directions, and in the distance he thought he could see a glimmer of light. He called out to the others that there must be a house not too far away. "Then we should go there," said the donkey, "because this accommodation is pretty poor." The dog thought a few bones and a bit of meat might do him good. And so they set out in the direction of the light, and as they drew closer, it became bigger and bigger and brighter and brighter, until they found themselves standing in front of the brightly lit house. It belonged to a gang of robbers. As the donkey was the biggest of the four, he crept up to the window and looked inside.

"Well, old Moldy-Mane, what can you see?" asked the rooster. "I can see a table full of delicious food and drink," replied the donkey, "with robbers sitting round it and enjoying themselves." "That would suit us nicely," said the rooster. "It certainly would, if we could get in there," said the donkey. Then the animals began to discuss how they could drive the robbers away, and eventually they came up with a plan. The donkey would stand with his front legs against the window, the dog would jump on the donkey's back, the cat would climb on top of the dog, and to finish it all off, the rooster would fly up and sit on the cat's head. As soon as they had done this, one of them gave a signal, and they all began to sing: the donkey brayed, the dog barked, the cat mewed, and the rooster crowed. Then they crashed through the window and into the room, accompanied by the clatter of broken glass.

On hearing this hideous noise, the robbers almost jumped out of their skins, thought they were being attacked by a ghost, and fled in terror out into the forest. The four friends now sat at the table, picked out whatever they fancied from the remains of the feast, and gobbled it up as if they hadn't eaten for the last month.

When they had finished, they looked for whichever kind of bed they each found most comfortable, and then put out the lights.

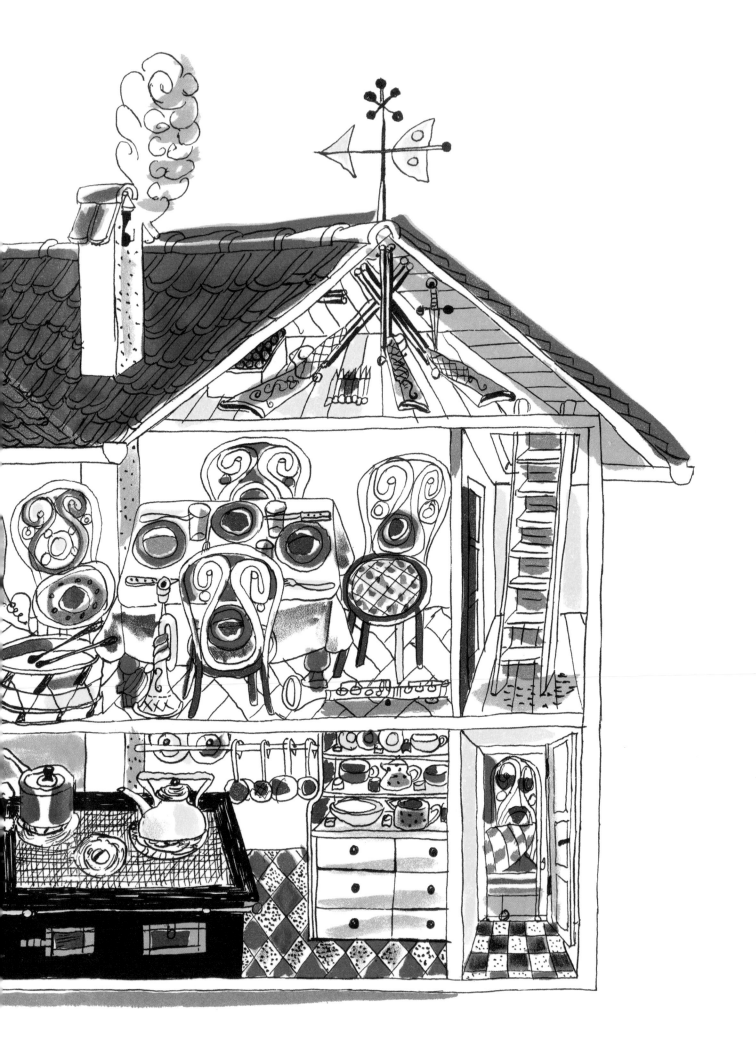

The donkey lay down on a pile of straw, the dog on a mat behind the door, the cat next to the fireplace near the warm ashes, and the rooster perched on the roof. As they were all exhausted after their long journey, they were soon fast asleep.

Just after midnight, the robbers saw from afar that the lights were out in their house, and everything was calm and quiet. "It seems to me," said the leader of the gang, "that maybe we shouldn't have panicked like we did." He sent one of his men to go and investigate. The man did indeed find that it was all calm and quiet. He went into the kitchen and lit a lamp. When he saw the blazing eyes of the cat, he thought they were burning coals and held out a match to light them.

The cat, who failed to see the funny side of this, leapt straight at his face, spat at him, and gave him a nasty scratch. The robber screamed, and in his terror rushed to the door, only to come face to face with the dog, who bit him in the leg. As he ran across the yard past the pile of straw, the donkey lashed out with his hind leg and gave him a mighty kick, and the rooster on the roof—having been woken up by all the noise—let out a deafening "cock-a-doodle-DOOOO!"

The robber limped back to his boss as fast as he could. "There's a vicious witch in the house who spat at me and scratched my face with her long fingernails, and the door is guarded by a man with a knife who stabbed me in the leg, and there's a dark monster in the yard that hit me with a wooden club, and up on the roof is the judge, who was yelling: 'Bring the criminal before me!' I was lucky to get away!"

From that moment onward, the robbers never dared to go back to their house, but the four musicians of Bremen were so happy there that they never wanted to leave. And as far as we know, they are still living there today.

Riff-Raff

One day the rooster said to the hen: "The nuts will be ripe now, so let's go to Nut Hill and have a feast before the squirrel grabs them all for himself."

"Good idea," said the hen. "Come on, then, we'll have a bit of fun together." Off they went

to the hill,

and as it was a nice sunny day, they stayed there till late in the evening.

Now it's hard to say whether it was because they'd eaten themselves to bursting point or because they were too snobbish, but the fact was they didn't want to walk home.

And so the hen built a little coach out of nutshells. When it was ready, she sat inside and said to the rooster: "Now you can harness yourself to it and take me home." "You must be joking," said the rooster. "I'd sooner walk home on my own than harness myself to this and pull you there. I never agreed to any such thing.

I'll gladly be the coachman and sit in the box seat,
but pull it I will not!"

While they were quarreling, a duck arrived. "Hey, you two thieves,"
quacked the duck, "who gave you permission to steal nuts from my
Nut Hill? Now you're going to pay for it!" She rushed at the rooster
with her beak wide open. But the rooster was a tough bird, and he
gave the duck a good beating, stabbing her so hard with his spurs that
she begged for mercy. As a punishment she agreed to let herself be
harnessed to the coach.

The rooster sat in the box seat and became the coachman, and off they set at a gallop. "Giddyup, duck!" cackled the rooster. "You can go faster than that!"

When they had traveled part of the way, they met two pedestrians, a pin and a needle. These called out to the coach to stop. They said soon it would be dark, they couldn't go a step farther, the road was filthy, and so please could they come and sit in the coach? They had been

at the Tailor's Inn near the city gate and had taken too long drinking their beer. As they were very thin and would not take up much space, the rooster let them in, but they had to promise not to step on his feet or those of the hen.

It was very late when they came to an inn. They didn't want to go any farther in the dark, and as the duck's feet were hurting and she kept flopping from one side to the other, they turned off into the courtyard.

At first the landlord made a big fuss, saying the inn was already full, and in any case he didn't like the look of the newcomers. However, after a lot of sweet talk—the promise that he could have the egg the hen had laid on the way and that he could keep the duck, which laid an egg every day—he finally agreed to let them stay the night.

Then they got him to serve them a nice, freshly cooked meal, and they feasted like kings.

Early next morning, before the dawn broke and while everyone else was still asleep, the rooster woke the hen, took the egg, pecked it open,

and the two of them had egg for breakfast. They threw the shell into the fireplace.

Then they went to see the needle, who was also still asleep, picked her up by the head, and stuck her in the landlord's cushion. And they stuck the pin in his towel. After that, without so much as a farewell crow or cluck, they flew away over the heath. The duck heard their wings whirring away, freshened herself up, found a stream, and swam down it—which was much quicker than pulling a coach.

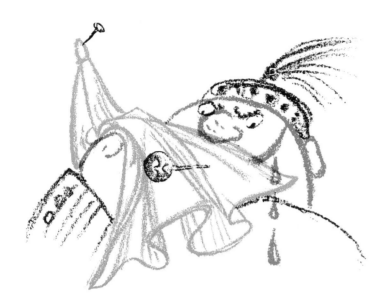

An hour or two later, the landlord climbed out of bed, had a wash, and started drying his face on the towel. But the pin went right across his face, leaving a red scratch from one ear to the other. He went into the kitchen and was going to light his pipe, but when he approached the fireplace, the eggshell leapt straight into his eyes.

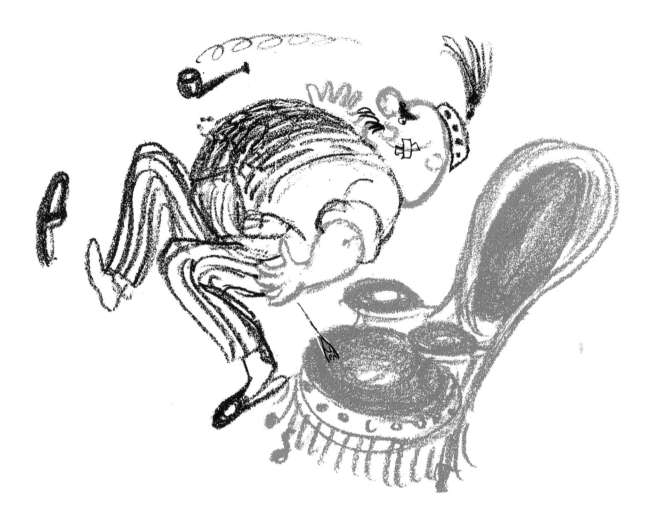

"Everything's stinging my head this morning," he said, and sank down miserably into his armchair. The next moment he leapt up with a cry of "OOOUCH!" The needle had given him the biggest sting of all, though it wasn't his head that had been stung!

Now he was furious, and he was sure he had been cheated by the guests who had arrived so late last night. But when he went to look for them, he found they had all gone. Then he swore that he would never again allow such riff-raff into his house. They ate everything, paid for nothing, and their thank-you present was to leave him their idea of a joke.

Rum-Pum-Pum

A Fairyland Parade

Puss in Boots

The Musicians of Bremen

Riff-Raff

King Easter Bunny

Death of a Chick

Rabbit and Hedgehog

The Seven Ravens

The Frog King and his Funny Acrobats

Puss in Boots

There once was a miller who had three sons, his mill, a donkey, and a cat. When the miller died, the three sons divided their inheritance: the eldest had the mill, the second son the donkey, and the youngest the cat and nothing but the cat. Then he was very sad and said to himself: "My brothers can use the mill for grinding and the donkey for transport, and will earn a good living between them, but what can I do with the cat? Should I kill him and make myself a warm cap out of his fur?"

The cat, however, was no ordinary cat and he had understood every word. He tried to comfort his poor master: "Don't be sad. Just have a pair of boots made for me and give me a bag that can be closed with a string, and then you'll see that things won't be so bad after all."

The miller's son didn't quite know what to make of this, but as the cat seemed to be rather clever, he took him to the shoemaker to be measured for a pair of boots.

What we are not told in the story is that it's far from simple for a cat to stand in boots and then to walk on two legs. He had to learn to do it, and so he practiced secretly at night—first standing, then walking, until finally he was able to do both.

When the cat felt safe walking on two legs, he picked up his bag and took it with him to the vegetable garden. There he put some carrots and some cabbage leaves in the bag and set off to the forest to hunt rabbits. He lay in wait for a while until a young and stupid rabbit came along to eat the nice food that was in the bag. *Swish!* The cat closed the bag with the string, and the rabbit was trapped. Then he put his catch on his back and took it to the palace to give to the King as a present.

On another day, he put some grains in the bag, went to a cornfield, and lay down pretending to be dead. Then he waited for some partridges to come along. And come along they did.

A nice fat partridge arrived and tried to peck at the grains. The cat swiftly closed the bag and again set off to give it to the King.

He could also fish, as all cats can, and when he caught a particularly large fish, once again he took it to the King.

This went on for several months. Every day the cat took whatever he'd caught to the King, and every day he would bow very low and say: "This is a gift from my master, Count Carabas."

The King greatly enjoyed eating the rabbit, the partridge, and the fish, and day by day became happier and happier, and fatter and fatter, and fonder and fonder of Count Carabas.

One day the cat said to his master: "Today you are going to make your fortune. All you have to do is go bathing. Leave the rest to me."

The cat had found out that the King and his daughter were planning to go for a ride, and one of their favorite routes was along the shore of the lake. The miller's son had now become used to taking his cat's advice, and so he undressed and jumped into the water. The cat hid his clothes under a big stone, and he had hardly done so when the royal coach arrived.

"Help! Help!" cried the cat. "My master is drowning!" When the King heard that and saw the cat, he immediately ordered the coachman to stop, because of course he recognized the cat who had brought him so many nice things to eat.

The cat told him that someone had stolen his master's clothes, and so the King sent one of his servants back to the palace to fetch some royal clothes for Count Carabas. The miller's son then put on these splendid clothes, and now he really did look like a count. The King graciously invited him to join himself and his daughter on their ride, and he was even allowed to sit next to the Princess, who was delighted.

What we are not told in the story and what is here revealed for the first time is how Puss in Boots spent hours in front of a mirror making horrible faces. Why? You will soon find out.

86

The cat ran on ahead and came to a big field where farmers were making hay. He called out to them: "Listen, all of you, when the King comes riding past and asks who this field belongs to, tell him it's Count Carabas's! If you don't, you will all die a painful death!" Then he pulled one of his horrible faces.

Soon afterward the King came by and asked the farmers: "Who does this beautiful field belong to?" "Count Carabas!" they all cried, because they were scared of the cat. The King congratulated the count on his beautiful field. The miller's son smiled a very modest smile. "What a fine fellow he is," thought the King to himself.

The cat had once again gone on ahead and came to a cornfield. "Listen, you reapers!" he said. "The King will soon come riding past. When he asks who this field belongs to, tell him it's Count Carabas's! If you don't, you will all die a painful death!" And he pulled another of his horrible faces.

Soon afterward the King came by and asked who the cornfield belonged to. "Count Carabas!" cried all the reapers, because they were scared of the cat. The King liked the count even more.

Again the cat had run on ahead, and this time he came to a castle that belonged to a giant.

What we are not told in the story is that the cat was a bit scared of the giant, and to boost his confidence, he had made himself look extra handsome.

The cat had made detailed inquiries beforehand and had found out that the giant was a great magician and was also extremely rich. He was the real owner of all the fields and forests through which the King had ridden. The cat sent one of the servants to inform the giant that he had not wished to pass by the castle without paying his respects to the most famous magician in the world.

Luckily the giant, who could sometimes be very nasty and bad-tempered, happened to be in a good mood when the cat arrived. He was practicing some new tricks, which he always enjoyed doing. The cat was very relieved that the giant was in a good mood, and he immediately began to talk about magic. "I've been told that you are the greatest quick-change artist in the world," he said.

"That's true," said the giant. "Take a look at my picture gallery. You'll see the animals I can change into." He was very vain and had had himself painted in all his different forms. "What would you like me to change into?" "An elephant!" cried the cat.

And straightaway he found himself face to face with an elephant, which even allowed him to swing on its trunk. "That's amazing!" cried the cat, but the next moment the elephant roared like a lion and—presto! He *was* a lion. "Unbelievable!" cried the cat, although secretly he was terrified. "But can you also change yourself into a small animal—a mouse, for example?" The lion roared: "Of courrrrrse!" and disappeared. Then the cat saw a little mouse scuttling across the floor. That was what he had been waiting for. With a single bound he jumped on the mouse and ate it.

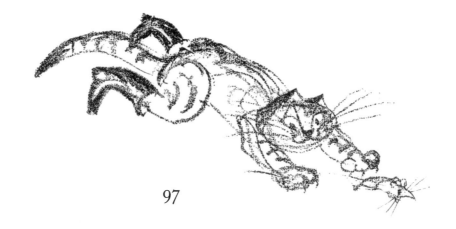

A while later, the King's coach arrived at the magician's castle. The cat hurried to the courtyard to greet the new arrivals. "Your Majesty, welcome to the castle of my master, Count Carabas!" The King was very impressed by the castle, which was even bigger and more beautiful than his own palace. The cat took everyone into the banquet hall. He had ordered the giant's servants—who were much happier to have him as their master than the bad-tempered giant—to prepare

a magnificent feast. The King was delighted, and thoroughly enjoyed all the food and drink. Obviously this Count Carabas had just about everything it took to be a member of the royal family, including the fact that he and the Princess couldn't take their eyes off each other. And so they were married on the spot, and even when day turned into night, they were still celebrating.

What we are not told in the story is that the cat was extremely happy when at long last he was able to take off his boots!

Fairy Tale Pictures

Red Riding Hood

There once was a sweet little girl who was loved by everyone who knew her, and especially by her grandmother. The grandmother was never quite sure what to give the little girl, but one day she gave her a cap made of red velvet, and it suited the girl so well that from then on she wore it all the time. And so she became known as Little Red Riding Hood.

One day her mother said to her: "Red Riding Hood, here's a piece of cake and a bottle of wine, and I want you to take them to Grandma. She's ill and weak, so this will make her stronger. You'd better go before it gets too hot, and be very careful how you walk, and don't leave the path. Otherwise you might fall down and break the glass, and then you won't be able to give it to Grandma. When you go into her bedroom, don't forget to say good morning to her, and don't start nosing around."

"Don't worry, I shan't do anything silly," Red Riding Hood promised her mother.

Grandma lived in the forest, about a half hour's walk from the village. When Red Riding Hood entered the forest, she met a wolf. But she didn't know that the wolf was a bad animal, and so she wasn't at all afraid. "I wish you good morning, Red Riding Hood," said the wolf. "Thank you, Wolf," she replied. "And what are you doing out here so early?" "I'm going to see Grandma." "And what are you carrying in your apron?" "Cake and wine. We did some baking yesterday, and so I'm taking this to Grandma because she's ill and weak and it will do her good and make her stronger." "And where does your grandmother live?" "About a quarter of an hour away in the forest. Her house is under three big oak trees with some nut trees around it. You must have seen it."

The wolf said to himself: "This young and tender thing is nice and meaty, and she'll certainly taste better than the old woman. But if you're really clever, you'll have them both." He accompanied Red Riding Hood for a while, and then said: "Look at those lovely flowers. You don't seem to notice any of the beautiful things around us. I don't think you've heard the little birds that are singing so sweetly. You just walk straight ahead as if you're going to school, but you're missing so many nice things out here in the forest."

Red Riding Hood now kept her eyes wide open, and when she saw the sun's rays dancing through the trees and lighting up the beautiful flowers all around, she thought: "If I take a fresh bunch to Grandma, it's sure to make her happy. It's so early in the morning that I'll still get there in good time." So she left the path and went off into the forest. And when she had picked one beautiful flower, she saw another farther away that was even more beautiful. And then another. Deeper and deeper into the forest she went, but in the meantime the wolf headed straight for Grandma's house and knocked on her door. "Who is it?" asked Grandma. "It's Little Red Riding Hood," lied the wolf, "and I've got some cake and wine for you. Please open the door." "Just press the handle!" shouted Grandma. "I'm too weak and I can't get out of bed." The wolf pressed the handle, the door opened, and in he went. Without saying a word, he went to her bed, opened his mouth, and swallowed her in a single gulp. Then he found some of her clothes, including a bonnet, put them on, got into the bed, and closed the curtains around him.

Red Riding Hood had been busy collecting flowers all this time. When she had gathered as many as she could carry, she set off again to take them to her grandmother. When she got there, she was surprised to find the front door open, and on entering Grandma's bedroom, she had a very unpleasant feeling. She thought to herself: "Dear Lord, why am I feeling so frightened? I always love coming to see Grandma." When she called out "Good morning," there was no reply. She went to the bed and opened the curtains. There lay Grandma, her bonnet pulled down over her eyes, and she really did look very strange. "Oh, Grandma, what big ears you have!" "All the better to hear you with." "Oh, Grandma, what big eyes you have!" "All the better to see you with." "Oh, Grandma, what a huge and horrible mouth you have!" "All the better to eat you with!" So saying, the wolf leapt out of the bed and swallowed poor Red Riding Hood in a single gulp.

With all that lovely food inside him, the wolf lay down on the bed again, fell fast asleep, and began to snore very loudly. A passing huntsman heard the noise and said to himself: "I've never heard the old lady snore like that before. I'd better go and see if she's all right." He went into the bedroom and saw at once that it was the wolf lying on the bed. "Now I've got you, you old rogue," he said. "I've been after you for a long time." He raised his gun and was about to shoot when the thought occurred to him that the wolf might have eaten the old lady, and she might still be alive inside him. Instead of shooting the wolf, he fetched a big pair of scissors and began to cut open the snoring animal's belly. After a few snips, he saw the red glow of the cap, and after a few more snips out jumped the little girl. "Oh, I was so frightened!" she cried. "It was pitch dark inside the wolf's belly!" A moment later, out came Grandma, who was still alive, though she could scarcely breathe. Red Riding Hood quickly fetched some large stones and put them inside the wolf. When eventually he woke up, he tried to jump out of bed, but the stones were so heavy that he simply fell back and died.

All three of them were happy now. The huntsman cut off the wolf's fur and took it home with him. Grandma ate the cake and drank the wine that Red Riding Hood had brought, and immediately felt a lot better. And Red Riding Hood told herself: "You must never again leave the path and go into the forest if your mother tells you not to!"

Lucky Hans

Hans had served his master for seven long years, and then one day he said to him: "Master, the time has come for me to leave you, as I would like to go home now and see my mother. Please may I have my wages?" His master replied: "You have been a good and faithful servant, and the reward should match the service." Then he gave Hans a piece of gold that was as big as his head. Hans wrapped it in a cloth, slung it over his shoulder, and set off for home. As he walked step by step along the hard road, a man came riding by, sitting calmly and comfortably while the horse carried him along at a merry trot. "Ah!" said Hans in quite a loud voice. "Riding is a wonderful thing. You sit up there as if you're in a chair, you don't trip over stones or wear out your shoes, and you don't even have to think about where you're going." Upon hearing this, the rider stopped and said: "Hey, Hans, why are you walking?" "I have no choice," said Hans. "I've got this heavy load to carry. It's gold, but it's so heavy I can't even hold my head straight, and it's also hurting my shoulder." "I'll tell you what," said the rider. "Let's swap. I'll give you my horse, and you give me your lump of gold." "I'll be more than happy with that," said Hans, "but I have to warn you, you'll find it very hard going." The rider climbed down, took the gold, helped Hans get into the saddle, put the reins in his hands, and said: "If you want it to go really fast, you have to click your tongue and shout 'giddyup'."

Hans was delighted to be sitting on the horse and trotting along without having to do anything himself. After a while, he decided he'd like to go faster, and so he started clicking his tongue and shouting "giddyup." The horse immediately set off at a gallop, and before he knew what was happening, Hans was thrown off and landed in the ditch that lay between the road and the fields. The horse would have galloped away if it hadn't been stopped by a farmer who happened to be coming along with his cow. Hans checked that all his limbs were intact, and then got to his feet unsteadily. He was now feeling very miserable and said to the farmer: "Riding is no fun at all, especially if you're sitting on a vicious beast like that, which jerks and throws you off so you almost break your neck. I shall never ride a horse again. But I really like the look of your cow. You can go for a leisurely stroll behind her, and every day she'll give you milk, butter, and cheese. What I wouldn't give to have a cow like that!" "Well," said the farmer, "if you really want to have her, I'll be happy to swap her for your horse." Hans was delighted with the offer, and so the farmer jumped up on the horse and galloped away, leaving Hans with the cow.

Hans gently drove the cow ahead of him and thought about the excellent deal he'd made. "If I have only a piece of bread, I still shan't be without a meal, because as often as I like I can have butter and cheese with it. And if I'm thirsty, I can milk my cow and drink as much as I want. What more can a man ask?" When he came to an inn, he had a break, happily ate the rest of his food—both his lunch and his supper—and spent his last penny on a glass of beer. Then he drove the cow on, heading for his mother's village. It was now almost midday, and the heat was becoming more and more oppressive. He reached a heath that would take about an hour to cross, and soon he was feeling so hot and thirsty that his tongue stuck to the roof of his mouth. "But I know just what to do," he said to himself. "I shall milk my cow and quench my thirst." He tied the cow to a dried-up tree, and as he didn't have a bucket, he held his leather cap under it—but no matter how

hard he tried, he could not get a single drop of milk out of the beast. His efforts were very clumsy, and the cow eventually lost patience with him and kicked him so hard on the head that he fell to the ground and for quite a long time had no idea where he was. Fortunately a butcher happened to pass that way, pushing a pig in a wheelbarrow. "What happened to you?" he asked, and helped poor Hans get to his feet. Hans told him, and the butcher handed him a bottle. "Have a drink," he said, "and refresh yourself. You won't get any milk out of your cow—she's too old. All she's good for is the slaughterhouse." "Oh dear," said Hans, rubbing his head, "who would have thought it? Of course it's good if you can have an animal to slaughter, but what sort of meat will you get? I'm not too fond of beef—it's not juicy enough for my taste. But if you've got a nice little pig like that . . . well, that would taste very different, and besides, you could also make sausages out of it." "All right, Hans," said the butcher, "I'll do you a favor. You give me the cow, and I'll give you the pig." "May God reward you for your kindness," said Hans. He gave the cow to the butcher, who untied the pig from the wheelbarrow and gave Hans the string by which it had been attached.

Hans moved on, thinking about how all his wishes seemed to be granted. Whenever something went wrong, it was immediately put right. Next he met a young lad who was carrying a beautiful white goose under his arm. They greeted each other, and Hans began to tell the lad about how lucky he'd been, and how he'd always managed to do such good deals with people. The boy told Hans that he was carrying the goose to a christening. "Just take it for a moment," he said, holding the goose by the wings, "and feel how heavy it is. We've been fattening it up for the last eight weeks. Whoever makes a roast dinner out of it will have to wipe the fat off both sides of his mouth."

"You're right," said Hans, weighing the goose in his hands, "it certainly is heavy. But my pig is no lightweight either." Now the boy looked round in all directions, shaking his head and with a worried expression on his face. "Listen," he whispered, "there may be something that's not quite right about your pig. In the village I've just come from, someone stole a pig from the mayor's sty. And I'm afraid, I'm really afraid, that this is the pig. They've sent people out to search for it, and you'd be in a lot of trouble if they caught you with it. At best you would end up in a dark dungeon." Poor Hans was now trembling with fear. "Oh dear God," he cried, "can you help me? You know better than I do what things are like around here. May I give you my pig in exchange for your goose?" "I'd be taking a big risk," said the lad, "but on the other hand I wouldn't want to be responsible for what they'll do to you." And so he took the string in his hand and quickly drove the pig away down a side path, while Hans, relieved of this latest problem, carried the goose under his arm and headed for home. "If I think about it," he said to himself, "I've actually got the better deal. First of all a fine roast, then all the fat that will drip out of it, which I can put on my bread for at least three months, and also the beautiful white feathers, which I can use to stuff my pillow to give me a good night's sleep. My mother will be so pleased!"

When he came to the last village, he saw a scissors-grinder with his cart and wheel, and as the wheel hummed, the man sang: "I turn the wheel and sharpen the steel, and wherever I go, I can earn a good meal." Hans stopped and watched him for a while. Then he said: "You must be doing well, as you're so happy at your work." "Yes indeed," said the scissors-grinder. "My work is as good as a goldmine. A true grinder is a man who can put his hand in his pocket at any time and pull out a fistful of money. But tell me, where did you buy that fine

goose?" "I didn't buy it," said Hans. "I got it in exchange for a pig."
"And the pig?" "In exchange for a cow." "And the cow?" "In exchange
for a horse." "And the horse?" "In exchange for a lump of gold as big
as my head." "And the gold?" "That was my wage for seven years of
service to my master." "So each time you've done pretty well for yourself," said the grinder. "But you'd really have made your fortune if you
got up every morning and heard the money clinking in your pocket."
"And how can I do that?" asked Hans. "By becoming a grinder like me.
And all you need is a whetstone—the rest is easy. Now, I just happen
to have a spare one. It's a bit damaged, so all I'd ask for in exchange is
that goose of yours. What do you say?" "Why do you even ask?" said
Hans. "I'd be the happiest man in the world if I always had money in
my pocket. Then I'd have no more worries at all." And so Hans handed
over the goose and took the whetstone in exchange. "Here it is," said
the grinder, handing him a perfectly ordinary but very heavy stone
that had happened to be lying on the ground beside him. "This is an
excellent stone. If you use it properly, even your old blunt nails will be
as sharp as new."

Hans loaded the stone onto his back and continued his journey with
a light heart and shining eyes. "I must have been born under a lucky
star," he said to himself. "Whatever I want I get." However, he had now
been on his feet since dawn, and he began to feel very tired. He was
also very hungry, because when celebrating his acquisition of the cow,
he had eaten all the food he had brought with him. He was finding it
more and more difficult to continue and had to stop every minute or
so to take a rest. And the whetstone seemed to be getting heavier and
heavier. He couldn't help thinking how much better off he would be
if he didn't have to carry it. At a snail's pace he dragged himself to the
side of a stream, with the intention of relaxing there for a while and

refreshing himself with the water. He knelt, and, without thinking, bent over to take a drink. The stone slid off his back and *splash!* Down it went into the water. He watched it sink, then jumped up with sheer joy that he was free of it. Then he knelt again and with tears in his eyes thanked God for showing him such favor and treating him with such kindness, freeing him from the stone that had been so heavy a burden. "There is no one in this world," he cried, "who is as happy or as lucky as I am!" And so with singing soul and dancing step he set out once more and never stopped until he reached his mother's house.

The Hare and the Hedgehog

This story, dear children, may sound like a piece of fiction to you, but it is true because my grandfather, who used to enjoy telling it to me, always said: "It must be true, my boy, because otherwise no one could tell it." Anyway, this is how it goes:

One Sunday morning in autumn, the buckwheat was blooming, the sun had risen in all its glory, the morning breeze wafted warmly over the fields of stubble, the larks were singing up in the sky, the bees were buzzing in the buckwheat, the people were walking to church in their Sunday best, and all the animals were happy, including the hedgehog.

The hedgehog was standing by his door with his arms folded, enjoying the morning breeze and singing a little song as well or as badly as any hedgehog might sing on a fine Sunday morning. While he was quietly singing to himself, it occurred to him that since his wife was washing and dressing the children, he might go for a short stroll across the fields and look at his turnips. These were quite near his house, and he and his family used to eat lots of them, so he regarded them as "his" turnips. No sooner said than done. He closed the front door and set off for the turnip field. He hadn't gone far and was just passing the sloe bush at the entrance to the field, when he met the hare, who was on a similar mission to inspect his cabbages. The hedgehog bade him a friendly good morning, but the hare—who considered himself to be a fine gentleman although in fact he was a nasty, pompous snob—did not return the greeting. Instead he looked down his nose and said: "What are you doing creeping round the field so early in the morning?"

"I'm taking a walk," said the hedgehog. "A walk?" sneered the hare. "It seems to me you could do better things with your legs than take a walk." This really annoyed the hedgehog, who could put up with almost anything except remarks about his legs, because he was aware that by nature they were crooked. "You seem to think you can do more with your legs than I can do with mine," he said. "I do indeed think so," scoffed the hare. "Then let's put it to the test," said the hedgehog. "I'll bet you that if we have a race, I'll beat you." "You must be joking!" laughed the hare. "You with your short, crooked legs can beat me? But that's fine with me if it's what you want. So what do you bet?" "A gold coin and a bottle of brandy," said the hedgehog. "Done," said the hare. "Shake hands on it, and let's start now." "Not yet," said the hedgehog. "There's no hurry. I haven't had breakfast yet. I'll go home first, have a bite to eat, and be back here in half an hour."

The hare was quite happy with this, and so the hedgehog left. On the way he thought to himself: "The hare relies on his long legs, but I'll find a way to beat him. He may be a fine gentleman, but he's also a silly ass and I'll make him pay for what he said to me." When he got home, he said to his wife: "Get dressed quickly, because you must come to the field with me." "What's going on?" asked his wife. "I've bet the hare a gold coin and a bottle of brandy that I can beat him in a race, and I need you to be there." "Oh, good heavens," said his wife, "have you gone crazy? How can you beat the hare in a race?" "Hush, my dear," said the hedgehog, "and leave it all to me. Hurry up and get dressed and come with me." What could Mrs. Hedgehog do? She had no choice but to follow him, whether she liked it or not.

On the way to the field, the hedgehog said to his wife: "Now listen carefully to what I tell you. We're going to run our race down that long field over there. The hare will run in one furrow, and I'll run in another, and we'll start at the top. Now all you have to do is hide at the bottom of my furrow, and as soon as the hare arrives at the end of *his* furrow, you call out: 'I'm here already!'."

They reached the field, and the hedgehog showed his wife where she was to hide. Then he walked up to the top of the field. When he got there, the hare was waiting for him. "Are you ready to start?" asked the hare. "Yes," said the hedgehog. Each of them took up his position in his furrow. The hare counted: "One, two, three!" and ran like the wind toward the other end. The hedgehog waddled a couple of steps, then ducked down low in his furrow and simply sat there.

When the hare finished his sprint to the bottom end, the hedgehog's wife called out: "I'm here already!" The hare could scarcely believe his eyes or ears. He had no doubt that it was Mr. Hedgehog because, as everyone knows, female hedgehogs look just like male hedgehogs. "There's something fishy going on here!" he complained. "I demand a rerun!" Then he and Mrs. Hedgehog took their marks, and once again he set off so fast that his ears could scarcely keep up with him. Meanwhile, Mrs. Hedgehog sat quietly at the bottom end of her furrow. When the hare reached the top, Mr. Hedgehog called out: "I'm here already!" The hare was now furious. "I demand another rerun!" he yelled. "No problem," answered the hedgehog. "As far as I'm concerned, we can have as many reruns as you like." The hare did seventy-three more reruns, and the hedgehogs had no trouble at all. Whenever he reached the other end, one or the other of them would simply announce: "I'm here already!"

On the seventy-fourth rerun the hare couldn't get to the other end. He collapsed to the ground halfway down his furrow, blood streamed out of his mouth, and he lay there as dead as a dodo. The hedgehog took his gold coin and bottle of brandy, called out to his wife to leave the furrow, and the two of them went home together as happy as hedgehogs could be. And if they haven't died yet, then they're still alive today.

That is the story of how the hedgehog ran the hare to death on Buxtehuder Heath, and ever since that day, no hare has ever agreed to race against a Buxtehuder hedgehog.

The moral of the story is, first, that no one, however fine a gentleman he may be, should ever make fun of someone beneath him, even if it is only a hedgehog. And second, if you want to get married, you should take a wife who is just like you. That is to say, if you are a hedgehog, you must make sure your wife is also a hedgehog, and so on and so forth.

The Brave Little Tailor

One summer morning, a tailor sat happily at his table by the window sewing away as hard as he could. A farmer's wife came down the street, crying: "Lovely jam for sale! Lovely jam for sale!" The tailor liked the sound of that, and so he stuck his little head out of the window and shouted: "Up here, dear lady, you can sell your wares up here!" The woman climbed up the three flights of stairs with her heavy baskets, and then the tailor made her unpack all the pots of jam. He studied them, lifted them up in the air, held them to his nose, and finally announced: "The jam seems good to me, so let me have four ounces, or if it's a quarter of a pound, that will be fine for me." The woman, who had been hoping for a much bigger order, nevertheless gave him what he wanted and left, mumbling angrily to herself. "May God bless this jam," said the tailor, "to make me big and strong." Then he went to the cupboard to get some bread, cut off a large slice, and spread the jam all over it. "This should taste nice and sweet," he said to himself, "but before I take a single bite I must finish sewing this waist-coat." He put the bread down beside him, went on sewing, and out of sheer pleasure made the stitches larger and larger. In the meantime, the smell of the sweet jam had wafted up the wall to where lots of flies were sitting. The scent was irresistible, and so they swarmed down and settled on the bread. "Hey!" yelled the tailor, "who invited you?" Then he chased the unwelcome guests away. However, the flies—who didn't speak his language—refused to be put off, and in fact came back with some of their friends. The tailor finally blew his top, as the saying goes, grabbed hold of a cloth, shouted, "This'll teach you!" and launched a brutal attack on them. When he finally stopped wielding the fatal cloth, he counted the dead: no less than seven flies lay motionless, legs outstretched, on the table in front of him. "What a hero I am!" he said, amazed at his own courage. "The whole town must hear about this." He quickly cut and sewed together a belt on which in large letters he embroidered the words: *Seven killed with a single blow!* "The town?" he continued. "No, the whole world should hear about it!" And his heart leapt with joy like a lamb in the meadow.

The tailor tied the belt round his waist and set out to travel the world, because he felt that his workshop was too small to do justice to such courage. Before he left, he had a look round the house to see if there was anything he wanted to take with him, but all he found was an old piece of cheese which he put in his pocket. Outside the town gate he saw a bird that had got trapped in a bush, and that too went into his pocket. Now he bravely marched along the road, and as he was light and nimble, he didn't feel at all tired. The road led him up a mountain, and when he reached the peak he came upon a mighty giant, who was sitting there quietly admiring the view. The little tailor cheerfully approached him and said: "Good afternoon, my friend. Am I right that you're simply sitting here looking at the great big world? Well, I'm on my way there to prove what I can do. Would you like to come with me?" The giant gave him a withering look and said: "You little lump! You miserable little clod!" "Enough of that!" said the tailor, and he unbuttoned his coat and showed the giant his belt. "Read this and you'll see what kind of man I am." The giant read it: *Seven killed with a single blow!* He thought it must refer to people the tailor had killed, which certainly demanded a bit more respect. However, he wanted to test him first, and so he picked up a stone in one hand and squeezed

it until water dripped out of it. "Now you do the same," he said, "if you're *that* strong." "Is that all you can do?" asked the tailor. "That's child's play for someone like me." He reached into his pocket, pulled out the old soft cheese, and squeezed it until the liquid dripped out of it. "Well?" he said. "A bit better than your little effort, don't you think?" The giant didn't know what to say because he still didn't believe that the little man could be that strong. He picked up a stone and threw it so high in the air that they almost lost sight of it. "Now then, you little squirt, see if you can do better than that!" "Good throw," said the tailor, "but your stone fell back to earth again. Now I'll throw one so high that it'll never fall back." He reached into his pocket, pulled out the bird, and threw it high in the air. The bird was delighted to be free, soared up and up, and never came back. "How was that, then?" asked the tailor. "Well, you can certainly throw," said the giant. "But let's see what you're able to carry." He took the tailor to a huge oak tree that had been cut down and now lay on the ground. "If you're strong enough," said the giant, "help me carry this tree out of the woods." "No problem," said the tailor. "If you put the trunk on your shoulders, I'll carry the twigs and branches, as they're heavier." The giant put the trunk on his shoulders, but the tailor perched on a branch, and as the giant couldn't turn to look behind him, he had to carry the whole tree as well as the tailor. The little man sat there cheerfully whistling the song called *Three Tailors Rode to the City Gate,* as if carrying a tree was the easiest thing in the world. After the giant had been dragging the heavy load for a short time, he had to stop. He called out: "Listen, I'm going to have to drop the tree!" The tailor swiftly jumped down, grasped the tree with both arms as if he'd been carrying it, and said to the giant: "You're supposed to be so big and strong, and yet you can't even carry a tree!"

The two of them walked on together and came to a cherry tree. The giant grasped the top of the tree, where the ripest fruits were hanging, bent it downward, handed it to the tailor, and gave him some cherries to eat. Of course, the tailor was far too weak to hold onto the tree, and when the giant let go of it, the tree sprang back up again, taking the tailor high into the air with it. When he fell back to earth—luckily without injury—the giant said: "Well, well, so you're not even strong enough to hold a few thin twigs!" "It's not a matter of strength," said the tailor. "Do you think something like that would bother a man who's killed seven with a single blow? I jumped over the tree because there are some hunters shooting down there in the bushes. Now jump over it yourself, if you can." The giant tried, but he could not jump over the tree and in fact became stuck in its branches, so once again the tailor had got the better of him.

"If you're so brave," said the giant, "come with me to our cave and spend the night there." The tailor had no objections and followed him to the cave. When they arrived, there were more giants sitting by the fire, and each one had a roast sheep in his hands and was busy eating it. The tailor looked round and thought to himself: "There's a lot more room here than in my workshop." The giant showed him a bed and told him to lie in it and go to sleep, but the bed was far too big for the tailor, so he crept into a corner instead. At midnight, when the giant thought the tailor was fast asleep, he got up, took hold of a big iron bar, and shattered the bed with a single blow. He reckoned that would finish off the little shrimp once and for all. At daybreak the giants went into the forest, having forgotten all about the little tailor. Then suddenly there he was, coming toward them, as cheeky and cheerful as ever. The giants, terrified that he would kill them all now with a single blow, ran for their lives.

The little tailor continued his journey, simply following his pointed little nose. After quite a while, he came to the courtyard of a royal palace, and as he was now feeling rather tired, he lay down on the grass and went to sleep. While he was lying there, people gathered round on all sides to read the words on the belt: *Seven killed with a single blow!* "Oh!" they said. "What is this mighty warrior doing here in our peaceful land? He must be a great lord!" They went and told the King, thinking that if war should break out, it would be very important and useful to have him on their side, and so under no circumstances should he be let go. The King regarded this as good advice and sent one of his courtiers with instructions to offer him a position in the army when he woke up. The messenger stood by the sleeping warrior, waited until the hero had stretched his legs and opened his eyes, and then delivered the message. "That is precisely why I have come here," said the little tailor. "I am ready to serve the King." He was received with great honor at court and given special accommodation.

However, the other soldiers resented the little tailor and wished he was a thousand miles away. "What's going to happen to us," they asked, "if we quarrel with him and he hits us? He'll kill seven of us with a single blow! Men like us wouldn't have a chance." They decided to go to the King and ask to be discharged. "We're in no condition to stand up to a man who can kill seven with a single blow." The King was sad that he was about to lose all his loyal troops for the sake of one man, wished he had never set eyes on him, and would very much have liked to be rid of him. But he didn't dare discharge him for fear that if he did, the man might kill him and his people and take the royal throne for himself. He thought long and hard about the problem until at last he had an idea. He sent a messenger to the tailor to inform him that since he was such a great warrior, he the King would make him an offer. In the forest there were two giants who were causing a great deal of trouble robbing and murdering people and setting fire to their houses. No one could even approach them without risking life and limb. If the tailor could conquer and kill them, the King would give him his only daughter's hand in marriage, with half the kingdom as a dowry. And he could take a hundred knights with him for support. "Not bad for a man like me," thought the little tailor. "You don't get offered a beautiful princess and half a kingdom every day." "Very well," he said, "I shall deal with these giants, but I shan't need the hundred knights. Someone who can kill seven with a single blow is not going to be afraid of two!"

The little tailor set out, followed by the hundred knights, but when they reached the edge of the forest, he told them to wait there. "I shall deal with these giants by myself," he said. Then he entered the forest, looking to the left and to the right. After a while he saw them both lying fast asleep under a tree and snoring so hard that the branches waved up and down with every breath. The nimble tailor filled his pockets with stones and climbed up the tree. When he reached the middle, he slid out onto a branch until he was sitting directly above the sleeping giants. Then one by one he dropped some stones on the chest of the first giant. He didn't feel anything initially, but finally the giant woke up, poked the second giant in the ribs, and said: "Why are you hitting me?" "You're dreaming," said the other. "I'm not hitting you." So they went back to sleep, and then the tailor dropped a stone on the second giant's chest. "What are you doing?" yelled the second giant. "Why are you throwing stones at me?" "I'm not throwing anything at you," growled the first giant. They moaned at each other for a while, but as they were both tired, they gave up and closed their eyes again. Then the tailor started his game once more. He picked out the biggest stone of all and hurled it down with all his might at the first giant's chest. "Now you've gone too far!" roared the first giant, jumping up like a madman and shoving the other giant so hard against the tree that it shook. The second giant did the same to the other, and the two of them were in such a rage that they started ripping out trees and hitting each other so hard and so often that eventually they both dropped dead at the same time. The little tailor jumped down from his tree. "Lucky for me that they didn't rip my tree out," he said, "or I'd have had to jump into another one like a squirrel. Not that I couldn't have done it." He drew his sword and slashed the chest of each giant a few times before returning to the hundred knights. "I've done the work—killed them both, though it was pretty tough going. They were so desperate that they pulled up some trees to try to defend themsel-ves, but it didn't help. You can't defend yourself against someone like me, who can kill seven with a single blow." "Aren't you even wounded?" asked one of the knights. "No, everything's fine," said the tailor. "They never touched a hair on my head." The knights didn't believe a word of this, and so they rode into the forest. There they found the giants lying in a pool of blood, with the uprooted trees all around them.

The little tailor duly asked the King for the reward that had been promised him, but the King now wished he hadn't made such a pro-mise and so once more he tried to think of a way to get the great warrior off his back. "Before I can give you my daughter and half the kingdom," he said, "you must perform one more heroic deed. In the forest there is a unicorn that is causing a lot of damage. I want you to capture it." "I'm even less scared of a unicorn than I was of the two giants," said the tailor. "Seven killed with a single blow—that's what I do." Armed with a rope and an axe, he set off for the forest and again told the accompanying knights to wait behind. It wasn't long before the unicorn arrived and came bounding toward him as if to stab him with its horn. "Easy, easy, not too fast," said the tailor to himself as he waited and waited until the unicorn was almost on top of him; then, with a single leap, he jumped behind a tree. The unicorn couldn't stop in time, crashed into the tree at full speed, and got its horn stuck so firmly in the trunk that it couldn't pull it out again. The unicorn was trapped. "Now I've got you," said the tailor, and he came out from behind the tree, put the rope round the unicorn's neck, and then used his axe to free the horn from the tree. When all this was done, he led the animal away and took it to the King.

However, the King was still reluctant to let him have the promised reward, and so he gave him a third task to perform. There would be no wedding unless he could first capture a wild boar that had also been causing great damage in the forest. This time he would have some hunters to help him. "No problem," said the tailor. "Child's play for me." He did not take the hunters with him into the forest, and they were pleased that he didn't, because they had encountered the boar several times before and had no wish to repeat the experience. When the boar saw the little tailor, it came running toward him with foaming mouth and razor-sharp teeth to try to knock him to the ground, but the nimble hero ran into a nearby chapel and then with a single leap jumped out again through a window. The boar chased after him, but he dashed round to the front and slammed the door shut. The raging beast was trapped, because it was far too heavy and clumsy to jump out of the window. Then the tailor called for the hunters so that they could see the trapped animal with their own eyes. Once more the tailor reported back to the King, who, whether he liked it or not, was now obliged to keep his word and hand over his daughter and half his kingdom. If he had known that it was a little tailor and not a great warrior that was standing before him, he would have been even more heartbroken. The wedding took place amid much splendor and little joy, and the tailor became a king.

One night, some time later, the young queen heard her husband talking in his sleep: "You, boy, make the waistcoat and patch the trousers, or I'll box your ears." Now she knew what the little man really was. The next morning, she told her father and begged him to help her find a way to be freed from her husband, who was nothing but a tailor. The King tried to comfort her and said: "Tonight leave your bedroom door open. My servants will wait outside, and when he's gone to sleep, they will go in, tie him up, and take him to a ship that will carry him far away." His daughter was happy with the plan, but the King's sergeant at arms, who had heard everything and rather liked the young lord, went and told him about the plot. "I'll soon put a stop to that," said the tailor. That evening he went to bed with his wife at the usual time. When she thought he was asleep, she got up, opened the door, and then lay down again. The little tailor, who had only been pretending to be asleep, began to shout in a clear voice: "You, boy, make the waistcoat and patch the trousers, or I'll box your ears. I have killed seven with a single blow, and killed two giants, captured a unicorn, and trapped a wild boar, so why should I be afraid of those who are standing outside my bedroom door?" When they heard the tailor say these words, the servants were terrified. They ran away as if they were being chased by an army of madmen, and none of them ever dared even to approach the little tailor again. And so he was still a king, and he remained a king for the rest of his days.

Hansel and Gretel

There was once a poor woodcutter who lived near the forest with his two children and their stepmother. The boy was called Hansel and the girl Gretel. They had very little to eat, and when the price of food suddenly increased, the woodcutter could not even afford to buy them their daily bread. One night he lay in bed wondering and worrying about what he could do, and he sighed and said to his wife: "What is to become of us? How can we feed the children when we don't even have the money to feed ourselves?" "I'll tell you what we'll do," answered his wife. "Early tomorrow morning we'll take the children to the thickest part of the forest. We'll light a fire for them and give each of them a piece of bread, and then we'll go to work and leave them there. They'll never be able to find their way home, and then we shall be free of them." "No, dear wife," said the man, "I'll never do that. How could I live with myself knowing that I'd left my children alone in the forest, where wild animals would soon come and tear them to pieces?" "You're a fool," she said, "because then all four of us will starve. All you can do is carve the wood for their coffins." And she would not let him rest until he agreed. "But I feel sorry for the poor children," he said.

In the meantime, the children were so hungry that they could not sleep either, and they overheard what their stepmother had said to their father. Gretel wept bitter tears and said to Hansel: "We're going to die!" "Shh, Gretel," said Hansel, "don't worry. I'll find a way to save us." When the father and stepmother were asleep, he got up, put

on his coat, opened the front door, and crept outside. The moon was shining brightly, and the white pebbles that lay in front of the house shone like silver coins. Hansel bent down and put as many as he could in his coat pockets. Then he went back into the house and said to Gretel: "Don't worry, my dear little sister, you can sleep peacefully now. God won't abandon us." And so saying, he lay down in his bed.

At daybreak, even before the sun had risen, the woman came to wake the two children. "Get up, you lazy creatures. We're going to the forest to get some wood." She gave each of them a piece of bread and said: "Here's something for your midday meal, but don't eat it before then because you won't be getting anything else." Gretel put the bread under her apron, because Hansel's pockets were full of stones. Then all four of them made their way to the forest. After a while, Hansel stopped and looked back at the house, and he did this over and over again. The father said: "Hansel, why do you keep stopping and looking behind you? Pay attention and don't forget what your legs are supposed to be doing." "Ah, Father," said Hansel, "I'm looking at my white cat sitting up on the roof. He's trying to say goodbye to me." "You little fool," snapped his stepmother, "that's not your cat. It's the morning sun shining on the chimney." But Hansel had not been looking at the cat. Each time he stopped, he took one of the shining pebbles out of his pocket and threw it on the ground.

When they reached the middle of the forest, the father said: "Now then, children, go and get some wood for me to make a fire so that you won't freeze." Hansel and Gretel gathered a pile of brushwood, which the father set light to, and the flames leapt high into the air. The stepmother said: "Lie down by the fire, children, and have a good rest while we go and chop wood. When we've finished, we'll come back and fetch you."

Hansel and Gretel sat by the fire, and at midday they each ate their piece of bread. They could still hear the sound of axe on wood, and so they thought their father was nearby. But it was not his axe at all. He had tied a branch to a withered tree, and the wind kept banging it against the trunk. After they had sat there for a long time, they were both very tired, and their eyes closed as they fell into a deep sleep. When they woke up, it was already dark night. Gretel began to cry and said: "How are we going to get out of the forest?" But Hansel reassured her: "Just wait a little while until the moon comes up, and then we'll find our way home." As soon as the moon rose, he took his sister by the hand and followed the trail of pebbles, which shone like new silver coins lighting up the way. They walked all night long, and at daybreak they were back at their father's house. They knocked at the door, and when their stepmother opened it and saw that it was them, she said: "You bad children, why did you sleep so long in the forest? We thought you would never come home!" But their father was overjoyed, because it had weighed heavily on his conscience that he had left them all alone.

Not long afterward, they were once more in dire need, and the children overheard their stepmother talking to their father in bed: "We're almost completely out of food again. There's just a half loaf of bread left, and that will be the end of us all. The children must go. We'll take them even farther into the forest so they'll never find their way out again. Otherwise we have no hope of surviving." The father was again very upset and felt it would be far better to share the last morsel with the children, but his wife would not listen to anything he said and mocked him and told him he was stupid. If you start with A, you must continue with B, and having given in once, he was forced to give in again.

Once more, however, the children were awake and overheard the conversation. When the grown-ups were asleep, Hansel got up with the intention of going outside and collecting pebbles again, but this time the stepmother had locked the front door and Hansel could not leave the house. Nevertheless, he reassured his sister: "Don't cry, Gretel. Go to sleep. The good Lord will help us."

Early next morning, the stepmother came and made them get up. They were each given their piece of bread, which was even smaller than the time before. On the way to the forest, Hansel kept his bread in his pocket and broke it into crumbs. He then stopped every so often to throw a crumb on the ground. "Hansel, why are you standing there looking behind you?" asked his father. "Just keep walking." "I'm looking at my dove sitting up on the roof," said Hansel. "She's trying to say goodbye to me." "You stupid boy," said the woman. "That's not your dove, it's the morning sun shining on the chimney." But Hansel went on throwing the crumbs on the path until they were all gone.

The woman led them farther and farther into the forest, to where they had never been before, and again lit a fire and said to them: "Sit down by the fire, children, and when you're tired, have a little nap. We're going to chop some wood, and when we finish in the evening, we'll come and fetch you." At midday Gretel shared her bread with Hansel, who had scattered his along the way. Then they went to sleep, and the evening passed, but nobody came to fetch them. When they woke up, it was dark night, and Hansel comforted his little sister: "Just wait, Gretel, till the moon rises, and then we'll see the crumbs of bread I scattered. They'll show us the way home." When the moon rose, they set out, but they could not find any crumbs, because the thousands of birds that lived in the fields and forest had eaten them all up. Hansel said to Gretel: "Never mind, we'll still find the way." But this time they didn't. They walked all night long and the next day as well, from dawn to dusk, but they could not find their way out of the forest. By now they were very hungry, because the only food they had was a few berries that had fallen to the ground. Eventually they were so tired that their legs could no longer carry them, and they lay down under a tree and went to sleep.

When they woke up, it was the third morning since they had left their father's house. Once more they set off, but simply went deeper and deeper into the forest. If they couldn't get help soon, they would die of hunger and thirst. At midday they saw a beautiful snow-white bird sitting on a branch, and it sang so sweetly that they stopped to listen. When it had finished, it swung its wings and flew on ahead, while they followed until they came to a tiny house. There it sat down on the roof, and when they came nearer the house, they saw that it was made of bread and had a roof of cake and windows of bright sugar. "Let's enjoy ourselves," said Hansel, "and have a really good meal. I'm going to eat a bit of the roof, Gretel, and you can have a window—that'll taste sweet." Hansel reached up high and broke off a piece of the roof to see how it tasted, while Gretel stood by a window and nibbled it. Suddenly, a gentle voice called out from inside:

"Nibble, nibble, like a mouse. Who is nibbling at my house?"

The children replied: "The breeze, the breeze, that blows through the trees."

Then they carried on eating as if nothing had happened. Hansel, who really liked the taste of the roof, tore a very large piece off it, and Gretel pulled a whole round windowpane out of the wall, sat down, and tucked into it. Then the front door opened, and out came a very old woman leaning on a crutch. Hansel and Gretel were so frightened that they dropped what they were holding, but the old woman simply waved her crutch and said: "Ah, you dear sweet children, who brought you here? Come in, come in and stay with me. Nothing nasty will happen to you." She took them both by the hand and led them into her little house. There she gave them lots of delicious food: milk, and pancakes with sugar, apples, nuts . . . Then she made up two little beds for them with shining white sheets, and Hansel and Gretel lay down in them, thinking they were in heaven.

But the old woman had only been pretending to be friendly. In reality she was a wicked witch who lay in wait for lost children and had built her little house of bread to lure them inside. Once they were in her power, she would kill them and eat them as a special treat for herself. Witches have red eyes and can't see very far, but they have a fine sense of smell, like some animals, and they can sense when people are approaching. And so when Hansel and Gretel had approached her house, she had laughed an evil laugh and cackled: "I'll have them, and they'll never leave here alive."

Early the next morning, before the children were awake, she got up, and when she saw them lying there so peaceful and innocent, with their round red cheeks, she murmured: "They'll certainly give me a good meal." Then she grabbed hold of Hans with her skinny hands, carried him into a little stable, and locked him in behind an iron gate. He screamed as loud as he could, but no one could hear him. Next, she went to Gretel, shook her awake, and snapped at her: "Get up, you lazy child. Go and get some water for your brother and cook him a nice meal. He's sitting outside in the stable, and I want him to get fat. And when he's fat, I shall eat him." Gretel began to weep floods of tears, but that didn't help her. She had to do as the wicked witch told her.

From now on, poor Hansel was given lots of lovely food, whereas Gretel had nothing but crab shells. Every morning the old witch hobbled over to the stable and said: "Hansel, stretch out your fingers so that I can feel if you'll soon be fat enough." But Hansel would hold out a tiny bone, and the witch—who was very shortsighted—couldn't see it properly, thought it was Hansel's finger, and was surprised that he wasn't getting any fatter. When four weeks had passed and Hansel remained as thin as ever, she became really impatient and was not prepared to wait any longer. "Come here, Gretel!" she shouted. "Go and get some water and hurry up. I don't care if Hansel is fat or thin, tomorrow I shall kill him and cook him." The poor little girl sobbed her heart out and the tears flooded down her cheeks as she brought the water in which he was to be cooked. "Dear God, please help us!" she cried. "If only the wild animals had eaten us in the forest, at least we'd have died together!" "Stop moaning," said the old woman. "It won't do you any good."

Early the next morning, Gretel had to hang the pot of water up and light the fire below it. "First we'll do some baking," said the old witch. "I've heated up the stove and kneaded the dough." She pushed poor Gretel toward the stove, where the fire was already blazing. "Get inside," said the witch, "and see if it's hot enough for us to put the bread in." Once Gretel was inside, the witch was going to shut the door, bake her, and eat her. But Gretel sensed what she intended to do and said: "I don't know how to do it. How can I get inside?" "You silly goose," said the witch. "The opening's wide enough. Can't you see? Even I could get inside it!" She went to the stove and put her head in the opening. Then Gretel pushed her as hard she could. The witch fell all the way in, and Gretel slammed the iron door and bolted it. *Aaaargh!* The witch began to howl quite horribly, but Gretel ran away, and the wicked old woman burned to death.

Gretel ran straight to Hansel's stable, opened the iron gate, and cried: "Hansel, we're free! The wicked witch is dead!" As soon as the gate opened, Hansel flew out like a bird from a cage. They were so overjoyed that they threw their arms round each other's neck, danced here, there, and everywhere, and kissed each other. Then, as they had nothing more to fear, they went into the witch's house. In every corner they found boxes full of pearls and jewels. "They're better than pebbles," said Hansel, filling his pockets, and Gretel said: "I want to take some home as well." She filled her apron with more of these beautiful things. "Now we must go," said Hansel, "so that we don't get lost again in the witch's forest." When they had walked for a few hours, they came to a big river. "We'll never get across it," said Hansel. "I can't see a crossing place or a bridge anywhere." "There aren't even any boats," said Gretel. "But there's a white duck swimming over there. If I ask it nicely, maybe it'll help us." And she called out: "Little duck, little duck, we're Hansel and Gretel. There's no crossing place and no bridge. Would you please carry us across on your white back?"

The duck swam toward them, and Hansel sat on its back and told his sister to join him. "No," said Gretel. "We'll be too heavy for the duck. It should take us across one by one." That is exactly what the kindhearted bird did. When they had reached the other side safe and sound, the forest began to seem more and more familiar to them, and at long last they saw their father's house in the distance. The poor man had not known one moment of happiness ever since he had left his children in the forest, but in the meantime his wife had died. He wept tears of joy to see them again. Then Gretel shook all the pearls and jewels out of her apron onto the floor, and Hansel took one handful after another out of his pockets. And so all their worries were over, and they lived happily and peacefully ever after.

The Seven Ravens

There once was a man who had seven sons but no daughters, though he greatly longed for one. At last, though, his hopes were fulfilled when his wife eventually gave birth to a little girl. They were overjoyed, but the baby was so small and weak that they were advised to have her baptized immediately. The father at once sent one of his sons to fetch some water for the christening, but the other six insisted on going with him. Each of them wanted to be the first to collect the water, and as they fought over the jug, it fell into the well. Then they stood there not knowing what to do, and they were all afraid to go home. When they failed to return, the father became impatient and said: "These ungodly children must have gone off to play some game and have forgotten what they're supposed to be doing!" He was afraid that the little girl would die without being baptized, and he was so angry that he shouted: "I wish all the boys would turn into ravens!" No sooner had he spoken these words than he heard a loud whirring sound in the sky above his head. He looked up and saw seven coal-black ravens, which flew round him and then away into the distance.

The parents could not take back the curse that he had put on them, and they were deeply saddened by the loss of their seven sons. However, they found comfort in their dear little daughter, who soon began to get stronger and became more and more beautiful with every day that passed. For a long time she didn't know that she had seven brothers, because her parents were careful never to mention them to her and had removed all trace of them, but one day by chance she happened to hear some people saying that although she was so beautiful, it was she who was responsible for the tragedy that had befallen her seven brothers. Then she was very unhappy, went to her father and mother, and asked if it was true that she had brothers, and if so, what had happened to them. The parents could no longer keep it secret from her, but they told her it had been God's will, and her birth had simply been the innocent cause. However, every day she suffered from deep pangs of conscience, and felt it was her duty to save her brothers. She could not rest, and so at last she crept away to search the world for her brothers and set them free, no matter the cost to herself. She took nothing with her except a little ring to remind her of her parents, a loaf of bread to satisfy her hunger, a jug of water to quench her thirst, and a little chair to rest her tired legs.

She walked on and on and on until finally she came to the world's end. There she met the sun, but it was too hot and terrible, and ate little children. She ran far away until she came to the moon, but it was much too cold and grim and ugly, and when it saw the child, it said: "I smell the flesh of a human being." She hurried away and came to the stars, and they were kind and friendly. Each of them sat on its own little chair, but the morning star stood up and gave her a chicken drumstick, saying: "If you don't have this drumstick, you will not be able to unlock the Glass Mountain, and that is where you will find your brothers."

The girl took the drumstick, wrapped it tightly in a little cloth, and continued on her way until she came to the Glass Mountain. The gate was closed, and she unwrapped the cloth, only to find that it was empty. She had lost the gift she had been given by the kind star. Now what was she to do? She was determined to rescue her brothers, but she did not have a key to the Glass Mountain. And so the faithful sister took

a knife out of her pocket, cut off one of her tiny fingers, put it in the lock, and opened the gate. When she entered the mountain, a dwarf came toward her and said: "What are you looking for, my child?" "I'm looking for my brothers, the seven ravens," she replied. The dwarf said: "My masters are not at home, but if you would like to wait here until they return, you may come in." The dwarf brought the ravens' food on seven small plates and their drink in seven small glasses, and the girl ate a crumb from each plate and drank a drop from each glass, but in the last glass she dropped the ring that she had brought with her. Suddenly there was a loud whirring and croaking in the air, and the dwarf said: "My masters are coming." Then in they flew, hungry and thirsty, looking for their plates and glasses. But one after another they cawed: "Who's been eating from my plate? And who's been drinking from my glass? This has been done by a human mouth!" The seventh, however, saw that at the bottom of his glass lay a ring, and he recognized it as having come from his father and mother. Then he said: "May God grant that our sister should be here, so that we may be free." When the girl, who had been standing behind the door listening to them, heard his prayer, she stepped forward, and at once the ravens were restored to their human form. Then they hugged and kissed, and happily made their way home together.

Hans Fischer, "Fis"

(January 6, 1909 – April 19, 1958)
Swiss artist, author, and illustrator of children's books

Hans Fischer was born in Bern, Switzerland. After studying art in Geneva and Zürich, Hans Fischer spent a year in Paris—employed by an advertising studio—before returning to Switzerland. There he worked on animated films, designed shop windows, and contributed regularly to various illustrated magazines. In 1933 he married Bianca Wassmuth, and they had three children, one of whom—Kaspar—also became an artist as well as an actor. In addition to his work for magazines, Hans created mural paintings for schools and for the Dählhölzli Zoo in Bern, stage sets for the Cabaret Cornichon, and a vast number of book illustrations. His fabulous creatures, always drawn with scientific precision, have enriched the imaginations of countless generations of children. He also wrote and illustrated the tale of *Pitschi,* a little cat that always wants to be something else. This was translated into many languages and became an international bestseller. Hans Fischer's work was displayed at many exhibitions and won numerous awards. He died from a heart attack at the age of forty-nine.

Sandi Paucic, 1998

Taken from: www.sikart.ch (SIKART encyclopedia and data bank of art in Switzerland and the principality of Liechtenstein) © Schweizerisches Institut für Kunstwissenschaft, Zürich and Lausanne)

First published in the United States, Great Britain, Canada, Australia, and New Zealand in 2018 by
NorthSouth Books Inc., an imprint of NordSüd Verlag AG, CH-8050 Zürich, Switzerland.

Distributed in the United States by NorthSouth Books Inc., New York 10016.

Library of Congress Cataloging-in-Publication Data is available.
ISBN: 978-0-7358-4339-4 (trade)
1 3 5 7 9 · 10 8 6 4 2
Printed in Latvia 2018
www.northsouth.com